The Circus under the Sea

Written by Mairi Mackinnon

Illustrated by Ben Mantle

How this book works

The story of **The Circus under the Sea** has been written for your child to read with your help. Encourage your child to read as much as they can, helping to sound out the words if they get stuck.

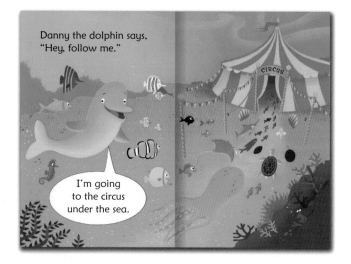

Danny the dolphin *says,* "Hey, follow me."

I'm going to the circus under the sea.

There are puzzles after the story, and for these you will need to read the instructions to your child.

You can find out more about helping your child with this book, and with reading in general, on pages 30-31.

The Circus under the Sea

Turn the page to start the story.

Danny the dolphin says,
"Hey, follow me."

I'm going
to the circus
under the sea.

Wendy the whale says,
"When will it start?"

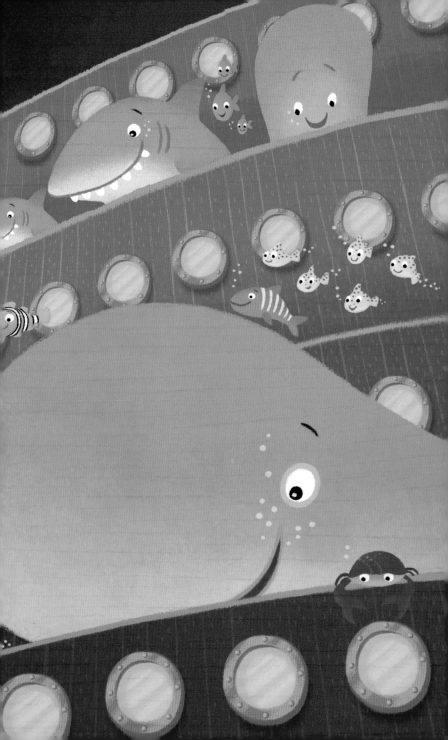

Is there a problem?
We hear a low moan.

"The stage lights are broken. Quick, lend me your phone."

Thank goodness! Here's
Eddy, the electric eel.

"I can fix them,"
he mutters. The
audience squeals.

It's showtime! The seahorses race around the ring.

The clownfish play tricks,

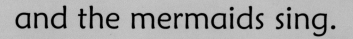

and the mermaids sing.

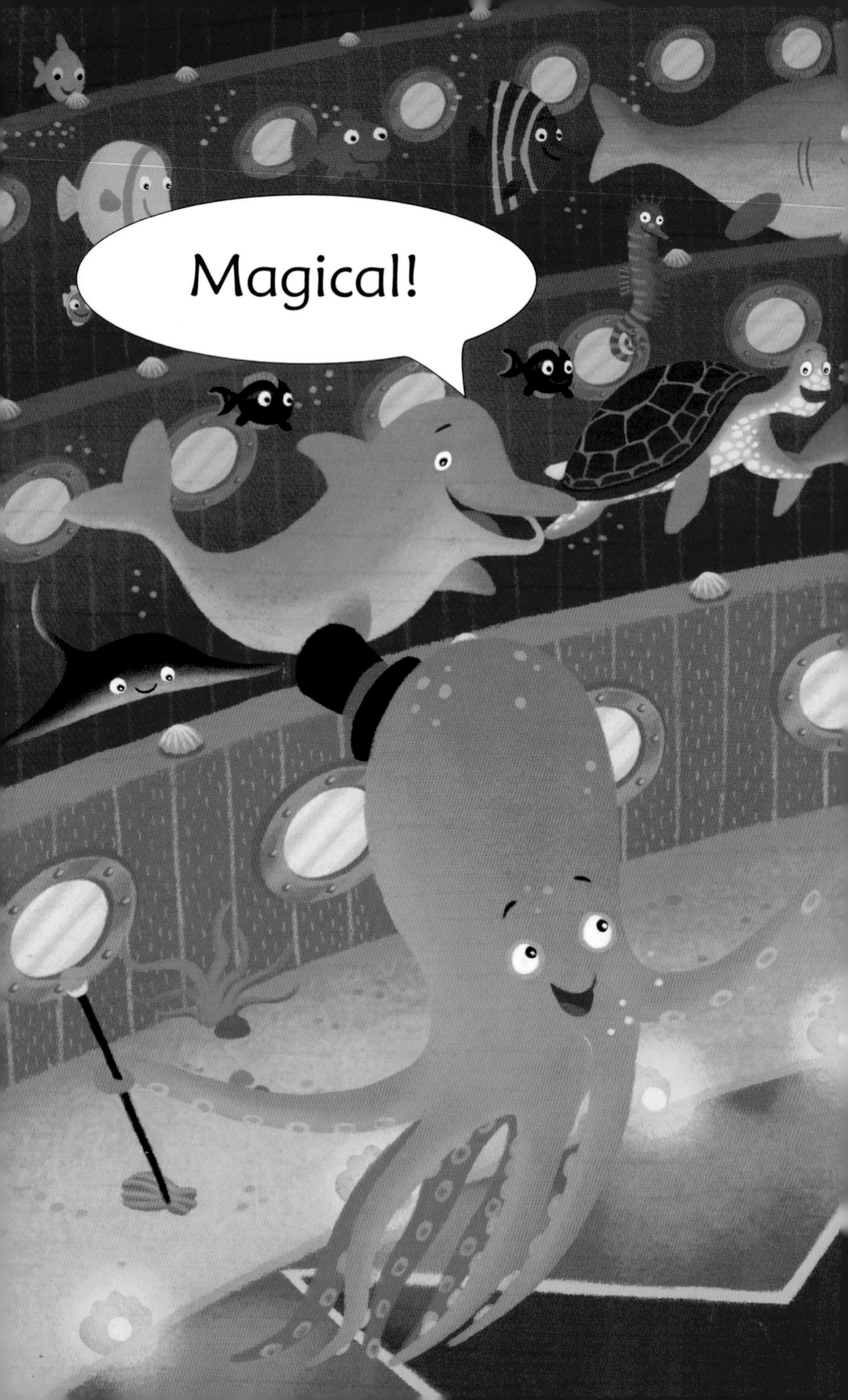
Magical!

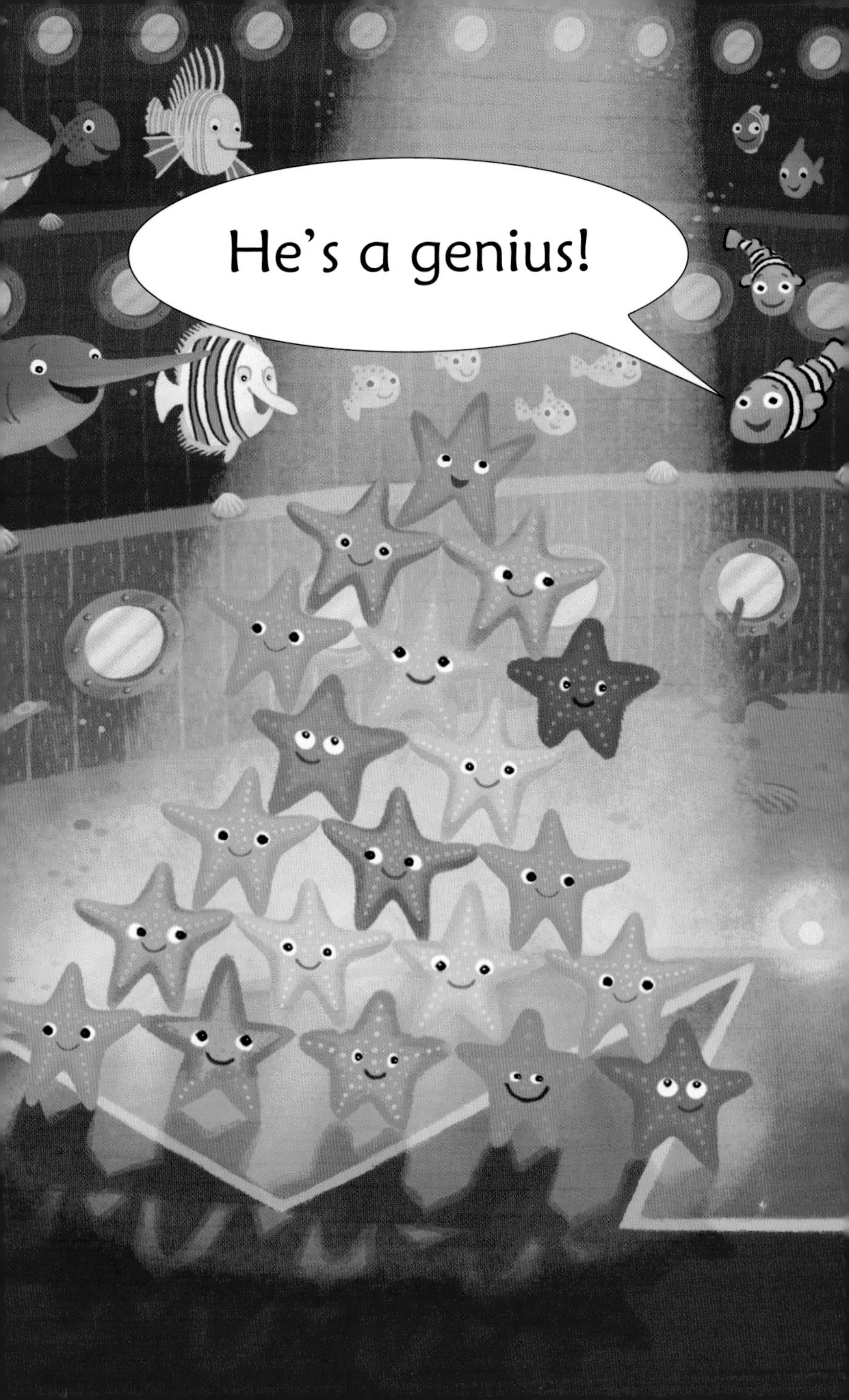
He's a genius!

The squid on the high
wire balance and sway.

But the real star is Eddy.
He saved the day.

Puzzle 1

Can you finish the sentences? Choose from the endings on the page opposite. (You can look back at the story if you need help.)

1.
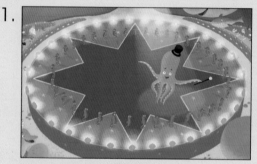

The seahorses...

2.
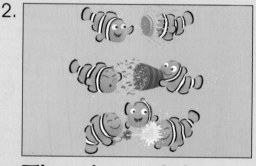

The clownfish...

3.

The mermaids...

4.

Eddy...

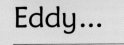

A   sing.

B   play tricks.

C   saved the day.

D   race around the ring.

Puzzle 2

Choose the right word to complete
each phrase.

1.

"Hey,......... me."

| help | copy | follow |

2.

Is there a .... ?

| practice | problem | prawn |

3.

"I can fix them," he ....

| butters | flutters | mutters |

4.

"................!"

| Magical | Medical | Musical |

Puzzle 3

Find the word in each group that begins with a different **sound** from the others.

1. | eel | each | every |

2. | circus | cactus | seahorse |

3. | fern | pain | phone |

4. | genius | jungles | goodness |

5. | howl | wheel | whale |

Answers to puzzles

Puzzle 1

1. D – race around the ring.
2. B – play tricks.
3. A – sing.
4. C – saved the day.

Puzzle 2

1. "Hey, <u>follow me.</u>"
2. Is there a <u>problem?</u>
3. "I can fix them," he <u>mutters.</u>
4. "<u>Magical!</u>"

Puzzle 3

1. every
2. cactus
3. pain
4. goodness
5. howl

Guidance notes

Usborne Very First Reading is a series of books, specially developed for children who are learning to read. **The Circus under the Sea** is the twelfth book in the series, and by this stage your child should be able to read the story alone, with occasional help from you.

The story of **The Circus under the Sea** introduces the following spelling patterns:

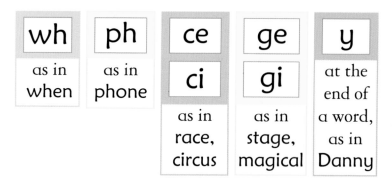

| wh as in when | ph as in phone | ce ci as in race, circus | ge gi as in stage, magical | y at the end of a word, as in Danny |

Later books in the series focus on letters that can be pronounced in different ways, while reinforcing the spelling patterns your child already knows.

You'll find lots more information about the structure of the series, advice on helping your child with reading, extra practice activities and games on the Very First Reading website,* **www.usborne.com/veryfirstreading**

*US readers go to **www.veryfirstreading.com**

Some questions and answers

- **Why do I need to read with my child?**
  Sharing stories makes reading an enjoyable and fun activity for children. It also helps them to develop confidence and stamina. Even if you are not taking an active part in reading, your listening and support are very important.

- **When is a good time to read?**
  Choose a time when you are both relaxed, but not too tired, and there are no distractions. Only read for as long as your child wants to – you can always try again another day.

- **What if my child gets stuck?**
  Don't simply read the problem word yourself, but prompt your child and try to find the right answer together. Similarly, if your child makes a mistake, go back and look at the word together. Don't forget to give plenty of praise and encouragement.

- **We've finished, now what do we do?**
  It's a good idea to read the story several times to give your child more practice and more confidence. Then, when your child is ready, you can go on to the next book in the series, **The Monster Diner.**

Edited by Jenny Tyler and Lesley Sims
Designed by Russell Punter

First published in 2010 by Usborne Publishing Ltd., Usborne House,
83-85 Saffron Hill, London EC1N 8RT, England. www.usborne.com
Copyright © 2010 Usborne Publishing Ltd.

USBORNE VERY FIRST READING

There are over thirty titles in the **Usborne Very First Reading** series, which has been specially developed to help children learn to read. Here are some of them.

To find out more about the structure of the series, go to **www.usborne.com/veryfirstreading**